Random Thoughts...
of a
Perplexed, Relaxed Soul

By
Christie C. Black

PublishAmerica
Baltimore

© 2008 by Christie C. Black.
All rights reserved. No part of this book may be reproduced, stored in a retrieval system or transmitted in any form or by any means without the prior written permission of the publishers, except by a reviewer who may quote brief passages in a review to be printed in a newspaper, magazine or journal.

First printing

PublishAmerica has allowed this work to remain exactly as the author intended, verbatim, without editorial input.

ISBN: 1-60441-558-4
PUBLISHED BY PUBLISHAMERICA, LLLP
www.publishamerica.com
Baltimore

Printed in the United States of America

I Dedicate
This Book to the
    Lover of my soul…
My friend…
    Comforter…
Dream releaser…
    Provider…
Protector…
    And father…
The Only True and Living God…
JESUS!!!

Acknowledgments

I would be remiss if I did not thank the Lord for giving me the ability, creativity, and time to write this collection of poetry. I also must give honor to the man and woman of God that Christ allowed to birth me into my dreams Dr. Marshall Mc Gill and First Lady Teresa Mc Gill. Of course I must acknowledge my mom an awesome motivator and encourager "love you to pieces". To my dad a man of few words when it comes to the "mushy" stuff but whether you said it or not I always knew you were proud. I must mention my brother thanks for your love and support. Thanks to KMWC for the gentle push towards putting my gift down on paper and the numerous prayers. To Markellia and Tonya thanks for being my sounding boards when I had to make sure every word was just right. To my WAS family thanks for the constant reminders to push towards my dreams.

Progression of Feelings:

Prologue 9
Love 11
Anger 21
Sadness 31
Joy 39
Confusion 47
Peace 57
Desire 65
Pain 73
Strength 79

PROLOGUE

Random Thoughts...

Different words run rampant through my soul...
    Yet unable to find their way out of my mouth...
Emotions...locked in my heart...
Afraid to share...afraid to start...
Opening up...who will receive...
What I have on my mind...
    The dreams unfulfilled...and vision concealed...
Can I be real???
    What would you say???
If I stand before you with all my imperfections...
All the flaws...and blemishes...the very things that you think should be in my past...
No...the true me...is subject to fall fast...
    But I'll get up...and I'll cover my indiscretions so that you can handle me...
So that you can feel like you know me...
    So that we can both be what others desire...never looking into one another's heart...
Never, seeing the ugly parts...Dealing with the surface...the place where things are safe...
Never will we face...the rambling that goes on in our head...
    The memories...the emotions...the fears...the hope...
Nope, they will continue to be random thoughts...

LOVE

From the Inside Out...

When you speak to me whether out of your mouth...or out of your spirit...
MY HEART LEAPS...
To lay in your arms...puts us in a world of our own...
MY SOUL REJOICES...
When you stand beside me we can take on the world...
MY PURPOSE IS AWAKENED...
As you look at me you see the innermost part that was hidden from the start...
MY EYES ARE OPENED...
When you hold my hands as they shake in fear and a calm falls on me just because you are near...
MY SPIRIT SMILES...
You have showed me
    Love in its purest form...
You have taught me...that it starts when spirits are aligned...
    You have changed me for the better...
And it is cause of you that I can love from the inside out...

I'm in Love...

Just got to tell ya'll
    About my man...
He is every woman's dreams...
    A friend when you need to share...
Your deepest secrets...never one to judge; but embraces you like it never happened...
    A lover not just of my physical body; but excites my emotions
And most importantly my spirit leaps...
    When I think about my man...
I'M IN LOVE...
Talk about a provider;
    He is richer than you could imagine...
As a matter a fact he is a King...
    As amazing as that seems...
He chose me...
    Cleaned me up...
Gave me new garments...
    Even changed my name...
Since the day he came...
    The new me could never be the same...
I'M IN LOVE...
    I know you want a man like mine...
And although he can be jealous...
    I wont be...
So on today fall in love with Jesus...
    JUST LIKE ME!!!!!!!

Breathe...

How do I describe or put into words...
Don't know if I can...Seems surreal this feeling that I feel...
Its like I've been holding my breath...
And now I can breathe...
Breathe in your air...
Inhale your essence...
Drown in your dreams...our dreams...
Visions of a future...Where we sustain...
Exist...have our being...Through each other...
Become one spirit...
One flesh...One heartbeat...
Where your breath becomes mine; as we intertwine...
AND JUST BREATHE...

Different…

Things are new; feelings hard to explain or express…
 However, in you there is something so different from the rest…
Your words are gently spoken…
 Providing comfort and peace…
God, has strategically placed you to eliminate my fears and help the hurt to cease…
 DIFFERENT…
We can talk for hours; and not want it to end…
 The most important part of it…you are a true friend…
Listening to the woos in my heart…
 Allowing me to have a fresh start…
Pulling me away from the hurts of my past…
 It is my daily prayer that this feeling would last…
There's something about you that has grasped my attention…
The very same thing dominates my thoughts…
Wondering where this path may lead…
 Knowing that you are the harvest of many a planted & nurtured seed…
 DIFFERENT…

A Love So Great...

Never would have imagined...
The joy that lives in my soul...
Or the smile that won't fade...
All the plans that we have made...
A love so great...
When I am in your arms...the time seems to stand still...
It is like it is all surreal...
This painting of my life...
    No more pain...no more strife...
A love so great...
I let you into my world...
    A privilege you have yet to take lightly...
But instead received me into your heart...
    Now it's like I can't breathe when were apart...
A love so great
    With each day...
As my comforter, encourager, and friend...
We grow closer still...
    So if I am dreaming...don't wake me...
Because I need you to be real...

I Never Knew Love…

Many times I searched for it…
    Around corners and different turns…
Behind doors and under hills…
While only finding cheap thrills…
Many times I looked for it…
In men or a quick hit…
Come to think of it…I never knew love…
Many times I created it…
By looking at who he could be and not who he was…
By settling for a warm body just because I never knew love…
Many times I searched the bottle…
Only to end of drunk and lonelier than before…
Hoping somewhere in that bottle was the big score…
The feeling that I longed for…
I never knew love…
Until Jehovah came in my life…
And loved me unconditionally…
Embraced me…shaped me sins and all…
He would even pick me up when I'd fall…
In him I got what I want and need NOT…search NO MORE CAUSE NOW I KNOW LOVE…

Our Relationship… (Dedicated to the Lover of My Soul)

It's like a courtship…
The nervous jitters…the butterflies in my stomach…
As I enter your presence…
I am so thrilled to kneel before you…
I am so privileged to be the apple of your eye…
As you look at me with pride…
    My heart swells…
As you tell me that I am fearfully and wonderfully made…
    I get chills…
To think that I have found favor in the eyes of the King…
    To think that my praise has brought a smile to your face…
That feeling could never be replaced…
    As we dance on golden sands…
You remind me of the virtuous woman that you see within…
This is so amazing it is hard to comprehend…
No longer servant but you call me "Friend"

ANGER

Blinding Shades of Red

Things I want to do to you…can not even be said…
I can hear them now…
She calls herself a "Christian"…
Maybe they've never been mad…
   Maybe they never felt like violence is the only choice they had…
Don't get me wrong???
The spirit is obedient; but that flesh is strong…
These blinding shades of red…
RAGE…escalates as my heart beats as if it is attempting to jump out of my chest…
   CALM DOWN!!!!!!…and do what's best…
The small voice whispers to my inner man…
Yet, I know if I get my hand on you!!!!!!!!
Boy this is out of control…
Adrenalin pumping…as I pace the floor…
Trying to calm down…trying to ignore…
Maybe it's because I trusted you…
Maybe it's the lies you told…
Maybe it's cause I couldn't handle all the control…
I don't know…but THESE BLINDING SHADES OF RED!!!!
Give me visions of you dead…
Is that something a "Christian" should have said…
This I don't know…but THESE BLINDING SHADES OF RED!!!!
Have got to go…

Untitled

This place is something serious...
    This feeling so strong...
It can barely be contained...
    How do you restrain???
When the one you thought was for you...has turned their back...
    Words were so sweet...
Gestures seemed so genuine...
    Now you've flipped...
Don't know if you're making the right choice...
    Don't know if your sure...
Were you sure when you took up my time...
    That I can't get back...
Or were you sure...
    When said you wanted to make it official knowing how I would react...
Just curious...
    If this decision is about me...
Or is it more about what's best for the man in the mirror...
    You tell me...
Sound angry, huh?
    Well, truth is I am...
Angry that you would come into my life...
    Turn it upside down...
With promises for a future...
    Fill my head with dreams of you and me...
Then change your mind...
    Want me to understand...
When what I want to do...is demand...
    Some answers to the many questions in my head...
But instead I hold my tongue...
    Give you space...
Lots of Space...cause I'm out!!!

What Do You Mean???

Pretend as if nothing happened...
Just move on girl...
At least you didn't get hurt...
I don't want to lead you on...
WHAT DO YOU MEAN??
You don't know what you want...
Didn't you know that up front...
How could you come in with promises of the world...
Now, you can't get your heart free from ole girl...
WHAT DO YOU MEAN???
Things seems so perfect...
I say all the right things...
It is almost like a dream...
Well, from the way you talk...it seems you must be woke...
Because this has got to be some kind of joke...
WHAT DO YOU MEAN???
Don't get this twisted...
We both talked hours on end about a future...
Nothing about let's just be friends...
No, it was not about sex...
But we were on a level greater than that...
My spirit lines up to yours in prayer on many a day...
Now you don't know if you can stay...
WHAT DO YOU MEAN???

What About Me???

Sometimes I wonder...
    What about me????
When it seems that blessings are not coming my way...
I struggle not to stray...
Constantly I pray...
    And seek your face...
Pursue your wisdom...
Inquire of your directions...and guidance...
    To no avail...
And on the inside I yell...
    WHAT ABOUT ME????
Even times I get angry...
    Then feel guilty for the anger...
At this stage my spirit is in the most danger...
Because in this place...I feel like a distant stranger...
No, longer your daughter...no longer a joint heir to the kingdom...
    No, longer full of purpose...no longer driven by my destiny...
LOST...LOST...NO LONGER FOUND...
And those words continue to resound...
    WHAT ABOUT ME???
What about my desires???
      What about my happiness???
What about the prophecies???
      WHEN GOD?? WHEN???
WHAT ABOUT ME????
It is in that place where it is the hardest to see...
    You working behind the scenes...because of all the smokescreens put in place by the enemy...
They come in the form of feelings that are difficult to manage...
    ENVY...
        LONELINESS...
            REJECTION...

               DEPRESSION…
                        BITTERNESS…
                                     BLAME…AND SHAME…
And too many more to name…
    So I've come to the conclusion…it is not an illusion…
And there is no confusion…as to whether you hear me…
And whether you see…
But if I choose to be stuck in…
    My "what about me???"
I will never see the true manifestation of the prophecies…

Hey You!!!!

I yell behind you as you close the door…
    Not just in my face…
But, on every dream that I made for our future…
    You say, "It's better this way."
I say, "Depends on who you ask…"
    No explanation…
        No rationale…
            No understanding…
Just OVER…OVER…
        Years I can never get back…
Tears so hot…
    Don't make any sense…
HEY YOU!!!
    Look at me…
Be a man…and tell me why????
    I gave you all of me…mind…body…and soul…
Still not enough…never enough…
        Wanted your freedom…
And I wanted you…
    Those didn't mix…
Tried to be what you needed…never getting that in return…
    Still I stayed…even laid down with you…
Innocence gone…seemed like a matter of minutes…
    Give it back…that precious part of me…
I yell…I scream…I cry…but nothing changes…
    Here I am…There you've gone…
With me yelling at your back…HEY YOU!!!

One of Those Days...

Sometimes I wake up...and I say this is one of those days...
    First of all my alarm does not go off...
    Then I hear the rain smacking against my window...
I think...man this sucks just got my hair done...
    Walk in the bathroom to take a shower...and room mate has used all the hot water...
    Finally, get dressed and step right in a mud puddle...
Thinking all the time... "I've had better days."
    Change clothes...get to work and realize I have to lead a meeting...
Walk in the room in front of all my colleagues...only to notice that my shirt is unbuttoned...
    "Can it get any worst???"
One of those days...
    After the 30th wrong number...and the 10th conference call...
I can finally leave...thinking..." things will be better once I am home."...
    Pull out of the parking space and SMACK!!! Someone hits me from the back...
Before I lose every semblance of a my creator...
    I yell to the top of lungs..."Just one of those days!!!"

SADNESS

Does Anybody Hear Me???

Distress written all over my face…
   Yet, I consistently replace it with a smile…
Anxiety is shown through my shaky hands…but still I continue to put my trust in man…
Anguish has become my closest friend…Somehow no one notices that it has all been pretend…
All a masquerade; a facade; a rouse; hoping no one will see the bruise after bruise…imprinted on my heart…
Yet, I scream on the inside as if being torn apart…
DOES ANYBODY HEAR ME!!!!!!!!!!!
Hear me crying out for help…
   Hear me begging for approval…
Hear the sad song on repeat in my soul…
NO, they never look that deep…
   Never seek to know all of me…
Never imagine that the bubbly smiley face that they see could really be…
A mask a shield to cover the tender part…
To protect the dreams, protect the destiny; protect the purpose…placed there by the hands of my creator…
Only to be released…to deserving ears…that will not only hear…BUT EMBRACE…

Listen, Baby…

How do I describe what I feel on the inside??
 How do I put into words the agony that has taken root in my heart???
How do I convey the ripping within my soul???
 Can you not see it??? Can you not feel my need to be near you; for you to embrace me…for you to say we're okay…
Could you possibly not share in my pain???
 Could you move forward as if there was never a you and me???
How could that be??? The idea of you turning your back to my tears…
 Shutting me out…all because of your fears…Fears that you will never be enough…
That I will desire you to be something or someone you just can't be…
 Did you ever think…that love covers…that love is patient…that love endures…
That love finds no fault…that love is vulnerability and faith wrapped in one…
PROBABLY NOT…that's why I am sitting in the midst of my tears…praying you through your fears…
 Believing that the holy spirit will whisper directions and purpose in your ears…
Listen Baby…

Stop the Rain…

Tears flow like rain…
    Drip…
        Drop…
On my heart they fall…
    Lord, don't let me build a wall…
A wall to keep out the pain…
    To close away the vulnerable feelings…
A shield to cover the sensitive parts of me…
    Even still the tears flow like rain…
How did we get here??? And how do we get back??? Or push forward?? I DON'T KNOW!!! Just goes to show the necessity for communication…
The very glue to hold any relation of two souls attempting to unite…
So what do we do???
        Answers unknown…
Until they are shown or revealed…
        The rain won't stop…

Frozen...

Something inside of you...
    Is Frozen in time...
You appear to be...so far from me...
Is your mind and heart in this very moment???
    How to get back???
How to defrost???
    How to come out of hiding???
How to break-free from fear???
    If only you had the answers...
If only you could grab hold to truth...
    Maybe then I could reach back...
Grab hold to the thoughts...the feelings that got me here...
      HERE??
It would appear that I could identify the place that I am in...
    Yet that is so far from true...
Actually, the place I am in...
    It's brand new...
You see this uncharted territory...at least with you as my co-pilot...
    We've never laid on this glacier...or made our home in an igloo...
No, our connection has been filled with sunny days...blissful evenings...
    And now I know that I need the snow to melt...maybe it has...
Or have my eyelids released the tears they have held captive???

Don't Look at Me...

Spirit man says go right...
    Yet, I continued my life to the left...
Striving daily to rectify all the sins of my past...as they continue to build a wall to block my future...
    I know that you pulled me out of my mess; but the flashbacks won't let me rest...
        DON'T LOOK AT ME!!!
When I stumble and fall far, far, far from your glory...
    When I give in to the thoughts of my flesh that have consumed my every action...
When I revert to the old man within...even though I put him off years ago...
    God, I can't take this no mo'
        DON'T LOOK AT ME!!!
In my heart I know the sacrifice that you made for me...
    But late at night when the enemy whispers sweet nothings in my ear...
My fear rises within that someone might hear...
    The pleasure I have as I give into the wiles of my emotions...
UP AND DOWN...back and forth...on one side to the other...
    Pushing me further away from your presence...
        DON'T LOOK AT ME!!!
I can't stand before you...Filthy thoughts, dirty hands, attempting to raise in praise...to the King of Kings...
    You know me...my thoughts, my secrets, my works, my deeds, my tears, my fears...
        PLEASE...PLEASE DON'T LOOK AT ME!!!!

Broken (7/4/07)

Time and time again...
    Always starts the same...
Full of great conversation...
    Full of compliments...
"You are the best." "Where have you been?"
Hearts knitted like the closest friends...
    Somewhere along the way...
Confusion comes...Fear rears its ugly head...
    Just when I think to fight; I wallow instead...
Broken...
    From dreams...
        To Hopes...
    Even Plans...
Everything that I saw for our life...
    Is now smeared...
        Is now blemished...
Torn...disconnected...subjected to ridicule
    This is how you left me...
To pick up the pieces...to give the right answers to all the questions that were to come...
    To be the voice of reason...To confront the critics...
    The resounding question is why...
        But there is no need to try to get a clear answer...
Which leaves me in the same space...Broken

JOY

On this Day!!! (3-23-07)

You handed me your heart...

As your knees shook...and your mind awaited the answer that lingered on my lips...

Lips that appeared to be frozen in time...

Desiring to respond yet...immobilized by joy, excitement, and fear...

Faith intervened as those three letters slipped out and tears welled...

Compelled by unrestrainable love we embraced...

As we attempt to gather our thoughts...

Suppress our beating hearts...

And come to grips with reality...

You for me and me for you...

FOR ETERNITY!!!

The Awakening (1/13/02)

I don't know what it was about that morning…
    But the sun seemed to shine a little brighter…
And my heart created a rhythm of its own…
    Even though I had set in that very pew…many…many times…
Did I say many a long drawn out Sundays…
    There was this pull almost magnetic…and I could no longer hold my seat…
But as if I were on auto pilot…
    I was up on my feet…
Somehow I got to the front…
    And to my surprise was even able to talk…
As the pastor welcomed me in…explaining how Jesus has erased my sin…
    Tears ran down my face…and immediately his love filled the void…
You know that empty space…
    No more slumber…
No more wandering…
    My eyes were opened…from the nightmare…known as my life…
As I embraced my awakening…

Simple Things...

A check in the mail...
    A call from an old friend...
A promotion on the job...
    Flowers from the one you love...
Birth of twin boys...
    Proposal to share his world...
Courtesy from a stranger...
    Hug from your grandma...
Kiss from your honey...
    Manifestation of a fervent prayer...
Cute picture by your five year old...
    A great book...
A bubble bath...
    Candlelight dinner...
A hilariously funny movie...
    And......just the simple things...

He Rose…

The sun shined brighter this morning…
    Something special about this day…
It was as if the grass was greener…
    The clouds looked softer than marshmallows…
And I looked up in awe and amazement…
    AS MY KING ROSE…
Rose from the gruesome death…
    That was predestined and had to unfold…
Rose with all power…
    Rose so that I could rise…
Out of pain…
    Out of shame…
Out of guilt…
    Out of condemnation…
Into joy…peace…strength…
    All because he rose!!

Destination Joy...

    A place of utopia...
A land of milk and honey...
    A setting of comforting things...
To some it's marriage...that place of safety and love...
    To others it's no responsibilities...
It may even be a sanctuary...
    Or the arms of him or her...
Could be the birth of your first born...
    Possibly never having to conform...
Wherever it is...
    However you get there...
        The question is how do you stay???
Will you even realize it if you have strayed away???
    What does it take to maintain??
This place of euphoria with no more pain...
    Is it only for the elite???
Do I have to compete or maybe it's a test I will have to complete???
    Can I drive???
Or must I fly??
    To this lofty place of a temporary high...
Maybe I am already there...
    But must embrace this stage...
Put away games, end the charade...
    Walk into the land in which my father has made...

CONFUSION

Crossroads...

Such a familiar place...
Yet a territory uncharted...
Almost like dejavu'
Or maybe just a full circle...
Circle of confusion, frustration, pleasure, and pain...
Crossroads...
Maybe I should toss a coin...
A coin to tell me where to go...
Yet within me the answer lies...
Under the tears, fears, self-pity, and shame...
In the midst of the illusion of a real life utopia...
Crossroads...
All signs point right: yet so intent...
On going to the left I am...
IN AND OUT...BACK AND FORTH...
Yes, no, maybe so...Heart racing...chasing...
A dream...a feeling...emotional high...
So hard I try...
To get there...
Crossroads...
Where is there???
Is it here???
Am I even near????
REVELATION, ANSWERS, WISDOM...
Or
Further, further away...drowning in guilt; shame; and blame...
CROSSROADS!!!

Forward...

How should I feel...
Sometimes the anger wants to erupt...
And pour out of me...like the lava that drips out of the mouth of a volcano...
Other times there is a smile on my face...that seems to be glued into place...
My mind wonders if this is the end...
Goodbye to possibility; goodbye to a friend...
Or maybe a beginning to a new chapter of a story...with many twists and turns and with each one...I hope to learn...
Learn how to love...
Not just how to feel...
Learn how to share...
Never to compare...
Loves that are lost...Loves that have gone away...Loves that have had their time and no longer can they stay...
As monumental moments...in my mind...
No, their time has expired...and although they have inspired...
Many articulate words...and eloquently spoken verses...
Still they can no longer inhabit my dreams...
No, it is time to clean out the corners of loves gone bad, erase the memories of men I've had...How should I feel or how will I feel...only time will tell...
But until then I will propel...FORWARD!!!

Am I Saved???

What does it mean??
Am I to be perfect???
Will my problems just cease??
These questions I pose to the father...
Where is this great joy???
How do I get my key??
You know the keys to my promises???
How does this worship thing work??
Am I supposed to still hurt???
Am I saved??
Salvation is just the beginning...
You still must choose...
Choose life or death...
NO, you will never be perfect, I am the only one...
Trails will come; so will errors...
Problems won't disappear...
But never you fear...
For your joy is here along with those keys...in my presence...There is peace and strength...Through your worship and praise...
That is what will get you through the days...

Mumbo-Jumbo

Mumbling…whispering…screaming words…rapidly racing in my mind…curved roads…crooked streets…
Unanswered questions…looks of dismay…
Desire to stray…pull to stay…
Right…NO, wrong way…NEW DAY!…
Not for me…blinded by darkness…
Unable to see…Future plans of good…Knowing what should…be done…
Playing and having fun…Boundaries crossed…
Hot then cold…struggling with the strongholds…
TIRED…sooooooooooooooooooo TIRED…
Release…Embrace…Washed away…and Erased…
Clean Slate…walking upright and straight…
LOOK BACK…turn around…
AM I LOST OR FOUND…
Confusion, Mania, Frustration, Temptation, Determination…
Tenacity; drives me toward the higher calling…answer me…
Answer me…cover ears to hear…open heart to listen…
Static loud; disconnect then reconnect…
Channel changed…deranged thoughts…
Tears suppressed…no rest…mind racing…yet pacing in and out…
Stableness needed…consistency succeeds it…submerged;
Pulled up; pushed down…
Life turned around…Stand your ground…
Rock and sway…come what may…But stay…
For this the day of…
CHANGE!!

Mixed Emotions...

Thoughts of you dominate my mind...
Feelings I cant control...
Happy, sad, mad, and glad...
All at once...Mixed Emotions...
Your smile does this thing to me...
Yet there's a side of you that I try hard not to see...
Face to face with you has my flesh elated...
But when I try to return to my true love...
My guilt has penetrated...my very being...
My worship I restrain...
Due to the pain...
I feel when I realize that yet again I've sinned and fallen short...
NOW WHAT?? Sit and cry...or shake it off and try again...
Again...and again...
Feelings out of control...happy sad, mad, glad...
Mixed Emotions...
What to do decisions must be made...
To step into the plan he laid...I know what to do...
Because my confusion is you...
My it: that thing to take me out of the will...
NO, I must stand still...
Feelings out of control...
Happy, sad, mad, glad...
Knowing what's right but looking, admiring, and even dreaming of the wrong...
I must stay strong...
It won't be long...
He promised great things...to those who wait...
Wait on him...the one who reigns...the one with the keys to all you need...
Want or could imagine...
So let go of your "it"...
No more confusion, no more illusion...Just stand and be PROVEN...
Feelings out of control...
HAPPY, SAD, MAD, AND GLAD...all at once...

I Can't Hear You...

Sometimes in the rain...
Through the fog...
Surrounded by pain...
I CANT HEAR YOU...
When my mind is changing like a remote control...
And the stressors of the day have taken their toll...
When my flesh is in the driver's seat...
And visions of my past are on repeat...
I CANT HEAR YOU...
Seems like I am running in place; when I attempt to seek your face...
It's like climbing a mountain...as I continue on this paper chase...
I CANT HEAR YOU...
It's like the voices in my head are on full blast...
How long will this feeling last...
Running through this black out...
I wish you would just shout...
So that I could hear your voice...
RECEIVE YOUR WISDOM...
    FIND SOME FREEDOM...
Trying to reach this kingdom...
Level of living...
    Oh, who am I kidding...
I cant get there...
    Oh, life is so unfair...
Being tossed and turned...here and everywhere...
I CANT HEAR YOU...
Unless I close my mouth...
    Open my heart...
Let you in...Cease to sin...then and only then will I hear you...

Don't Know If You've Been There...

A place of emptiness, a drought, a barren land; my very own lodebar...seemingly no answers...Screams go unheard...Tears fall on the hearts of the unmoved...emotionless creatures...
Who will turn their back to your distress...Who don't even blink as your heart is slowing being ripped out...
Don't know if you've been there...
When you knock until your knuckles bleed...
But no one answers...
You wonder if they are enjoying your pain...
You wonder if in some sick, misconstrued way your sorrow is their source of joy...
Maybe I am the only one...who has cried until there were no more tears...
Held hands with all of my fears...Embraced my disappointments...and became captive to my failures...
I tiptoed in the direction of self-destruction all the time looking for a way out...
Some sign of hope...A place of safety...Someone who is all KNOWING...needing to be made aware of the good that lives within me...
All the time he was there...ushering me through these trials...
Leading me as the dog leads his blind owner...
Allowing me to endure...
Molding me in the fire...
Shaping me through each iniquity...
Maturing me in the midst of each delay...
Picking me up after each fall...
So that I might stand tall before you...
Having endured the test...which are now testimonies of his goodness...
Acknowledgements of his faithfulness...
So yes, I've been there...and now I am here...
Just to remind you...no matter the situation...
GOD IS NEAR...

PEACE

Fresh Wind...

Blowing softly on my face...
Gently whispering words of freedom...
Barely audible sounds of deliverance...
Fresh wind...
Infuses me with power and strength...
Girds me up with holiness...and righteousness...
Restores the love that was lost...Seals our bond like never before...
Fresh wind...
Comes right when you need...
Only if you are open to receive...
Helps you to conceive...
All the dreams...visions...prophecies...
As he breathes...A FRESH WIND...

I Found Myself...

Wandering around many times in circles...
    Down roads with dead ends...
Connecting with the wrong friends...
    Drowning in the abyss of bad choices...
Smothered by the troubles of the world...
    I found myself...
Somewhere in the midst of lies and deceit...
    Underneath condemnation and defeat...
Covered in lust; engulfed in pain...
    Stranded in a place of constant rain...
    I found myself...
And when I did...
    I didn't recognize my exterior for
It reminded me of a kid...
    Naïve and gullible; fragile & torn...
Used and confused; hurt & ashamed...
    Tired of all the tricks; tired of the games...
So I brought you this broken shell of me...
    You embraced me as if I were a beautiful sight to see...
You cleansed me; made me new...
    Erased my past and pushed me to...
The one who you designed with a specific purpose in mind...
    The one who you created for this very time...

When I Enter

I lift my hands…to surrender to your will…
I open my mouth…to praise who you are…
I run in place or all around to give you glory…
I clap my hands…to exalt you as KING…
I wave my arms from side to side to worship you…
I bend down on my knees to show my reverence…
I dance before you to show you my heart…
I moan and groan…to utter the cries of my soul…
I kiss your feet…to show you that I am humbled before you…
I give you all of me…because I don't know any other way…
To enter your throne room…
To come before your throne of grace…
To lay in your holy place…
To stand before your face…
Whisper my deepest fears…
Knowing that you hear me…
When I enter…
    When I enter…

Comforting...

A gentle breeze...
    A soft embrace...
        Waves caress the ocean's edge...
Raindrops tapping the window's ledge...
    Melancholy tunes tickle my eardrums...
Intimate time with my creator...
    COMFORTING...
A hug from a dear friend...
    The softest lyrics in my ear...
        Absolute silence...
The perfect stanza to end a thought...
    Calming peace; after we have fought...
    COMFORTING...
The smell of fresh cut grass...
    The sounds of toddlers when they laugh...
        A baby being rocked to sleep...
A saxophone player in key and on beat...
    COMFORTING...

Our Place

We have a place where we can meet…
    Where I can lay at your feet…
Inhale your sweet aroma…
    Dance in the arms of the lover of my soul…
Whisper all my hurts; cry out praises…make my petitions known…
    OUR PLACE…
A set apart area…
    Where the love is far more than any can measure…
Where my inhibitions know no limit…
    Where my dreams are revealed…
        Where you restore me…
            Where you hold me up…when I am at the end of my strength…
    THIS IS OUR PLACE…
In this space…my mask is removed…
    You see my inner parts…and you smile…
Because regardless of what I see in the mirror…
    You know that I am all you created me to be…
You reveal in part…the many plans…that you have for my life…
    IT IS IN OUR PLACE…
That I am no longer afraid…
    But I am released from fear; no more depression; or oppression…
No, I am at liberty to be all that you called me to be…and as I dance before you…
And sing the love song to you my king…
I know that I am made whole…
    IN OUR PLACE

Nothing Broken; Nothing Missing

Coming into the fullness of who I am in you...
Truly comprehending the love that you have for me...
The opening of my eyes to the favor that you have placed in my life...
Understanding that before I am anyone's partner in the natural I am first your wife...
Nothing broken; nothing missing...
Feeling complete and whole through the love that you show me...
Embracing all that you predestined me to be...
Releasing the hurt...forgiving my past...allowing restoration to take place...
Dismissing destructive thoughts...so I can see all the more clearly your face...
Nothing broken; nothing missing...
Lack in no area...the search for peace now over...
For I have found my place of sanity...
A place full of relief...
All encompassing is the tranquility...
With nothing broken; nothing missing...

DESIRE

I Need You...

    How can you not know??
You make me whole...
    How can you not know??
Time goes by but without you it seems to stand still...
    How can you not know???
That the tears won't stop...
    That I can not breathe...
That my heart aches...
    That my body is limp...
Without you...
    How can you not know????
How much I need your touch...
    How much I miss your kiss...
How much just your voice soothes my soul...
    Could you know???
And not care and not hurt as I do...
    And not feel my tears...
        And not want to hold me as I you...
Is that possible???
    To know my need and turn away...
No...not you...anybody but you...
    The love of my life, my friend, my counselor, my past and future...
You couldn't know, but
    HOW COULD YOU NOT KNOW???

Forbidden...

You shouldn't do that...or say that...or go there...
That's not right...
You know your wrong...
Ringing in my ear...FORBIDDEN...
Pulling me, tugging me, towards you...that thing...my it...that blocks...STOPS...and hinders my surrender...
    Forbidden...
Maneuver my mind; block out...the thoughts: speak the word...
All these remedies I've heard...
Over; and over even in my sleep...
    FORBIDDEN...
Face to face...decisions at hand...
Commanding my flesh to withstand...
Overriding my emotions...
There must some kind of potion...
To stop the ache...so that I can shake it...
Forbidden...
    Hold on tight to his promises...
Stay in his will...
Don't trust how you feel...
    But kneel...
Before him...reveal your heart...a good start to push...pass the Forbidden...

My Passion...

You are the air that I breathe...
My very reason for living...
The source that provides...
Our love no one can divide...
My Passion...
You give my heart joy...
And my soul a new song...
In your presence is where I belong...
I don't think it could be any stronger...This pull towards your throne...
This draw to worship...
This desire to look into your eyes...
My Passion...
You have given me everything...
Yet you ask for nothing in return...
But I devote all of me...
As I bow my head...
Lifting my heart...It is in you that my life finally starts...
My Passion...
It is there at your feet...
That I can show you who I am...
NO, need to put on airs...
   No restraint if people stare...
All I care about is loving on you...
My Passion...
That is where I am complete...
Worshipping you is a feeling no one can beat...
Being made whole...
   Allowing you to fully take control...
So even when the world is weighing heavy and taking it toll...
Things will only get better...
As I hold on to you...
MY PASSION...
   MY PASSION...
      MY PASSION...

Songs Within...

    I have a pull to release...
All that is within...
    Line upon line...
Stanzas that never end...
    When I pick up my pen...
It's as if it moves on its own...
    Creating worlds that I've never witnessed...
Dreams that have been reoccurring...
    Articulately expressing pain and love...
Symbolically depicting my king...
    Dramatically interpreting places I have seen...
Healing me slowing with each curve of the letters...
    Freeing me from anger and placing me at peace...
That's why I push to get to my paper...
    I always carry my pen...
Cause I desire to reach those things...so that the songs within
    Will be released along with you and me...

Girl Talk

    Did you see him??
How could I miss???
    Such a fine specimen
You know my mind quickly went to martial bliss...
    There you go...is that all you think about...
What else is there??
    Now you are not being fair...
You know there is so much more...
    Pour your life into a child...
Maybe music, dance, or poetry...
    Better yet...Why don't you find a good ministry??
One where your time is more productive...
    And maybe you won't feel so incomplete...
Girl, all I can see right now...is how can I compete...
With the next woman...
    Cause I can't imagine living my life alone...
Who said anything about being alone...
    I am talking about peace, unconditional love, a lover like no other, a friend to the fatherless...
WHERE YOU ASK??
    1-800-JESUS

PAIN

I Hurt

I don't know how to make it stop...
As much as I need you...
　I also need to stay away...
Come to me...
　Hold me and make it stop...
Take the pain away...
　Wipe the tears as they flow...
Slowly they flow down...
　You have been my friend, lover, and at times as close as a brother...
Where do I go from here??
　How do I close the door??
The door that only you have the key to...
　The door to my soul...every vulnerable part of my being...
I must make the pain stop...
　I must find closure...
I must no longer hide...but confide in my true friend, the lover of my soul...
　I must trust his way is right...
No longer put up a fight...
　I must take up his burden and yoke for they are light...
I hurt...
　But it won't be long...
Until I will be singing a new song...
Song of joy, peace, and love...
　A song of freedom from all of the hurt!!!!!!!

Piece Me Back Together

I don't know how to gather myself…
Like pieces of a puzzle spread out on the floor…
Really can't do this no more…
Scattered here and abroad…
Are little fragments of my heart…
Dispersed are my emotions which have gotten away from me…
Need your spirit to collect all the bits that I so freely gave away…
Don't really remember the hour, the season, or even the day…
Could you please piece me back together????
Like the carpenter that your are…
Like the healer that you've proved to be time and time again…
Like the one who restores…and never changes…from beginning to end…
And even in the midst of it all you still call me friend…
Sometimes I wonder
If it is even possible…
Could I ever truly be whole…
Yet there is this voice that whispers softly…
I AM the only one you need…
And if you call upon me I will hear you…because I cannot fail but ONLY succeed…
And I will piece you back together…
Not only that…but it will be your greatest comeback…
You will soar like an eagle…or stand ever so tall and regal…
Everything that you felt you lost…
I will give back double…
Collecting; Shaping; and Molding you anew…
So well that you will forget all the trouble you've been through…
So to answer your question… "Can I make you whole?"
I will simply remind you that no matter how things look I have always been in CONTROL….

When I Hide Myself, Inside Myself...

No one can hear me crying out...
    No one knows how I want to shout...
It is almost like there is no more pain...
Yet in my heart it continues to rain...
When I hide myself; inside myself...
No one can see me for who I am...
I become a shell of normal woman...
I melt into others image of me...
But no one ever truly sees...
When I hide myself; inside myself...
The rejection doesn't hurt so bad...
I don't even have to be sad...
Even though my smile is plastered on as if I am glad...
No one really cares though...
They all ask the right questions...
Say all the right things...
Continue to move through a daily routine...
When I hide myself; inside myself...
No one sees my flaws...
    No one sees the fragmented person...I've become...
And I can remain numb...
When I hide myself; inside myself...

How Could You Love Me???

When you called me; I didn't answer...
    Instead I turned my back...
Turned from the very things you wanted to do for me...
    To all the things you tried to protect me from...
I neglected our time together...
    Even stopped coming to your house...
The very friends you separated me from...
    I ran to be in their company...
Giving them all your time and all your money...
    Used the body that was created to worship you...
To fulfill others carnal lusts...
    Yet through it all...
You continue to show me love like I've never known...
    That very concept is impossible to comprehend at times...
A love without bounds...
    A love without limits...
A love that requires nothing; yet has given everything...
    I don't deserve that type of love...after all that I daily do to reject it...
Yet you so freely embrace me; forgive me; and ask me to stay...
How could you love me...when I continuously turn away...

STRENGTH

This Too Shall Pass...

When situations seem out of control...
    All the doors that you desire to be opened...seem to be sealed...
Every prophecy and direction has yet to be revealed...
KNOW THAT THIS TOO SHALL PASS...
Walls seem to be closing in around you...
Dreams seem to fade away...
The hand of the Lord seems to not want to stay...
Your mind says stray...this saved thing aint for you...
KNOW THAT THIS TOO SHALL PASS...
Crying becomes a daily routine...
No one seems to hear your pain...
Getting out of bed becomes more of a strain...
Distant from everyone is how you feel...
Emotions are harder and harder to conceal...
KNOW THAT THIS TOO SHALL PASS...
Yet, you wonder how, when??
Is it something I must do to stop the hurt...
A soft voice whispers let me love you...from the inside out...
You want to shout...or maybe just pout...cause you don't know how to give it up...
So finally, no more tears...you just stand in awe...
    And wait...
        For the manifestation
            With a new determination
KNOWING THAT THIS HAS ALREADY PASSED!!!!!!!!!!!!

Created for Battle...

I've given you the weapons...
To fight this fight...
I created you victorious in your own right...
See I birthed you as a solider in my army...
Even before your mother conceived you in her womb...
You were predestined to wage war against all enemies...
And no, it's not the faces that you see everyday...
It is the spirit behind them...
That sets out to push you away...
Away from my plan for you...
Away from the purpose within...
    Away from dreams that you have yet to comprehend...
Don't worry you have tools...
    I've given you the armor...
You are equipped...cause I created you for battle...

It Came at a Price...

It came at a price...this thing called freedom...
BLOOD; SWEAT; TEARS...
Long nights full of fears...
Fear that it was your night to be the master's delight...
Fear that your time of reigning in Africa would only be a distant memory far from sight...
IT CAME AT A PRICE...this thing called freedom...
From Martin's march...to Rosa's refusal to give up her seat...
From Malcolm's demise...to the innocent look in the eyes of our little brown babies as we explain...
"White only" restrooms or why you were beat with brooms...chased by dogs...put into jail...squirted with hoses...
All for this thing called "Freedom"...
See it came at a price...this thing called Freedom...
When they stretched our savior wide...
When they beat him unmercifully...and the bruises were more than they could hide...
But they did not want to...NO...
They wanted you to see...So that TODAY...we would know...
THAT IT CAME AT A PRICE THIS THING CALLED "FREEDOM"...
In hopes that we would embrace each other as a people...
That we would exercise our right to vote...
That we would take advantage of every educational opportunity...
That we would hold our heads high...
Knowing the struggle...
Identifying with the inner strength...
Displaying the demeanor of royalty...
Embracing and Walking into all of the privileges of this "Freedom"
...For it came at a price...this thing called "Freedom"
BLOOD, SWEAT, TEARS...

What Do We Do Now???

When it seems like all is lost...
    When your worst nightmare is reality???
When there are so many unanswered questions???
    WHAT DO WE DO NOW???
Do we turn our backs on hope???
    Nope, these options just wont work...
    WHAT DO WE DO NOW???
Maybe we pick up an old vice...
    Or run away wouldn't that be nice...
Should we find someone to blame...
    Or build a wall to cover out hurt and pain...
    WHAT DO WE DO NOW????
We must find comfort in the word...
    Hold tight to every memory or dream deferred...
Embrace the peace found only in our maker...
    Take a gut check of our lives to be sure there are no deal breakers...
To hinder our reunion on the other side...
    Where our souls can meet again and harmoniously reside...
Now that we know what we must do...is save our goodbyes...and replace them with our see you later...
    For we are striving to live a life where we will one day met our creator!!!!

My Ancestors

Wisdom pours out of their mouth…
    Direction permeates from their soul…
All the struggles have made them stronger…
    Their life is a road map to our future…
Out of their seed we were given our very being…
    Their hearts are filled with love for the generations to come…
        Their laughter is music to my ears…
MY ANCESTORS…
    Strong they have been…
Courageous they were…
    Victorious always…
        MY ANCESTORS…
            MY ANCESTORS…
                MY ANCESTORS…

Speak...

Willing I am...
To be used...
Worth is something...
I don't feel...
But, righteous you have made me...
So I must be...
Humble I am...
In your presence...
As you speak through my lips...
Words of wisdom...
Words of power...
Words of deliverance...
Only as I bend to surrender
To your will...
Attempting to fulfill
Your purpose...
Your plan...
I know that I am but a man...
Yet when you stand within me...
There is a freedom...
That escapes my vocal cords...
With such fiery
It can not be ignored...
So I explore...
And implore...
For more of you...
Deliverer, friend, King...
Although sometimes I turn away...
Still you stay...
And use me...
To speak your words...not only to locals but so much more...
As I pour

Out my heart to the nation...with a determination...no hesitation...
Because the one who stands and speaks
IS A NEW CREATION...

About the Author:

Christie C. Black is an innovative and inspiring author. She graduated from Morris Brown College, Atlanta, GA with a BS in Psychology. In addition, she completed her MS in Community Counseling from Troy State University, Phenix City, AL. She currently lives in Columbus, Georgia where she was born and raised. Upon completion of her MS she pursued licensure as licensed practicing counselor(LPC). Currently, she is pursuing a certification in school counseling with the anticipated completion of May 2008. Through her clinical experience she utilized poetry as a medium to aid individuals in their journey towards healthy emotional development. Additionally, as Christie walks with God she has been able to enfuse her poetry and creativity as an instrumental part of her ministry. It is her hope that each reader will experience the emotion that was poured into each line and stanza of this collection of poetry.